S0-ADB-801

JUNIOR BRAVES OF THE APOCALYPSE

BOOK 1: **A BRAVE IS BRAVE**

ONI PRESS

AN ONI PRESS PUBLICATION

JUNIOR

OF THE APOCALYPSE

BOOK 1: **A BRAVE IS BRAVE**

WRITTEN BY
Greg Smith &
Michael Tanner

ILLUSTRATED BY
Zach Lehner

BRAVES

LETTERED BY
Jared Jones &
Christopher Sebela

EDITED BY
Charlie Chu

DESIGNED BY
Hilary Thompson

PUBLISHED BY ONI PRESS, INC.

JOE NOZEMACK • FOUNDER & CHIEF FINANCIAL OFFICER

JAMES LUCAS JONES • PUBLISHER

CHARLIE CHU • V.P. OF CREATIVE & BUSINESS DEVELOPMENT

BRAD ROOKS • DIRECTOR OF OPERATIONS

MELISSA MESZAROS • DIRECTOR OF PUBLICITY

MARGOT WOOD • DIRECTOR OF SALES

RACHEL REED • MARKETING MANAGER

AMBER O'NEILL • SPECIAL PROJECTS MANAGER

TROY LOOK • DIRECTOR OF DESIGN & PRODUCTION

HILARY THOMPSON • SENIOR GRAPHIC DESIGNER

KATE Z. STONE • GRAPHIC DESIGNER

SONJA SYNAK • JUNIOR GRAPHIC DESIGNER

ANGIE KNOWLES • DIGITAL PREPRESS LEAD

ARI YARWOOD • EXECUTIVE EDITOR

ROBIN HERRERA • SENIOR EDITOR

DESIREE WILSON • ASSOCIATE EDITOR

ALISSA SALLAH • ADMINISTRATIVE ASSISTANT

JUNG LEE • LOGISTICS ASSOCIATE

SCOTT SHARKEY • WAREHOUSE ASSISTANT

ONI PRESS, INC
1319 SE MARTIN LUTHER KING, JR. BLVD
SUITE 240
PORTLAND, OR 97214

ONIPRESS.COM
FACEBOOK.COM/ONIPRESS
TWITTER.COM/ONIPRESS
ONIPRESS.TUMBLR.COM
INSTAGRAM.COM/ONIPRESS

THATAMAZINGTWIT.TUMBLR.COM / @THATAMAZINGTWIT
DINERWOOD.BLOGSPOT.COM / @MIKEISERNIE
@2AMAZINGWRITERS
ZLEHNER.COM / @ZLEHNER

First Edition: July 2015
Second Edition: August 2018

ISBN 978-1-62010-526-9
eISBN 978-1-62010-145-2

JUNIOR BRAVES OF THE APOCALYPSE: A BRAVE IS BRAVE, August 2018. Published by
Oni Press, Inc. 1319 SE Martin Luther King Jr. Blvd., Suite 240, Portland, OR 97214. JUNIOR
BRAVES OF THE APOCALYPSE is ™ & © 2018 Greg Smith and Michael Tanner. All rights
reserved. Oni Press logo and icon ™ & © 2018 Oni Press, Inc. All rights reserved. Oni Press
logo and icon artwork created by Keith A. Wood. The events, institutions, and characters
presented in this book are fictional. Any resemblance to actual persons, living or dead,
is purely coincidental. No portion of this publication may be reproduced, by any means,
without the express written permission of the copyright holders.

Printed in China.

Library of Congress Control Number: 2015900806

1 3 5 7 9 10 8 6 4 2

This book is dedicated to the memory of Frank Smith.

Thank you for marking the path.

✕

A BRAVE
IS BRAVE

CHAPTER ONE...

DAY 1.

THEY'RE
LATE.

NOOB TUBED!

TRAVIS, ARE YOU DRESSED?

YES.

WE'RE GOING TO BE LATE. WHERE'S YOUR BROTHER?

HE'S ON THE PORCH.

IS HE READY?

I DON'T KNOW. MARVIN, ARE YOU READY?

I'M READY.

MROW

THEY DON'T EVEN SAY A PRAYER AT THE START OF JUNIOR BRAVE MEETINGS. THERE ARE NOT EVEN ANY OTHER LUTHERANS! THAT'S WEIRD!

LUCAS, SWEETIE, WE KNEW THINGS WOULD BE DIFFERENT IN ROSELAND. YOU SOUND LIKE YOU DON'T EVEN WANT TO GO ON THIS CAMPOUT.

OF COURSE I WANT TO GO! I CAN EARN AT LEAST FOUR SKILL PATCHES ON THIS CAMPOUT.

THAT'S KIND OF A BIG DEAL.

JOHNNY, THIS IS GOING TO BE AN EMPOWERING EXPERIENCE FOR YOU. YOU KNOW, CULTURALLY.

YOU GET TO SPEND SPRING BREAK AT CAMP BOBCAT! THAT'S EXCITING.

JOHNNY, THIS IS IMPORTANT... CULTURALLY.

YOU ALREADY SAID THAT, HENRY.

WELL, IT IS!

JOHNNY, SWEETIE, CAN YOU AT LEAST TRY TO MAKE SOME FRIENDS?

MY SON IS STILL A LITTLE BOY. HE'S MY LITTLE BOY--

AWWW, "LITTLE BOY." THAT'S PRECIOUS.

MOOOOM!

YOUR DELICATE SNOWFLAKES WILL BE FINE. THE VAN LEAVES IN FIVE MINUTES.

BE AN EXAMPLE AND HAVE FUN.

I BET WE DON'T EVEN SAY A PRAYER.

WHY DON'T YOU OFFER TO LEAD IT?

BE GOOD, PRABIR! REMEMBER MOMMY LOVES YOU!

ALL RIGHT, YOU BOYS THINK YOU ARE READY?

WE'RE READY, PADRE. "A BRAVE IS BRAVE" RIGHT?

WHO HAS A CELL PHONE OR A GPS OR A GAMEBOY OR ANY OTHER SUCH DOOHICKEY?

TOSS 'EM IN.

HEY, WHERE'S BUDDY?

SORRY I'M LATE. MY CAR WOULDN'T START SO I HAD TO BORROW MY ROOMMATE'S BIKE.

UM, HEY GUYS.

HI BUDDY.

TRIBE LEADER SIR, I THINK BEFORE WE GET STARTED, MAYBE WE COULD SAY A PRAYER?

I COULD--

DYLAN, AS PEYAK PATROL LEADER WHY DON'T YOU LEAD THE PRAYER? AMIR, YOU CAN SIT THIS ONE OUT. PRABIR, YOU TOO.

IT'S COOL.

OKAY.

DEAR JESUS, PLEASE PROTECT US ON THIS CAMPING TRIP.

AMEN.

AND WE'RE GOOD?

YOU STILL HAVE KEYS?

THEY NEVER ASKED FOR THEM BACK.

YOU SURE YOU'RE UP TO THIS? I DON'T KNOW HOW MUCH TROUBLE YOUR HIP IS GIVING YOU.

YEAH, I'M FINE, PADRE. THIS HIKE IS NOTHING. WE'RE JUST GOING TO CAMP BOBCAT, RIGHT? RIGHT?

RIGHT?

THIS ISN'T WHERE WE'RE SUPPOSED TO BE.

DUDE, QUIT WHINING. I SWEAR IF IT'S A WEEK OF THIS MOMMA'S BOY--

TRAVIS, CHILL. DON'T BE A JERK ON DAY ONE.

WHATEVER.

DYLAN, YOU'RE PATROL LEADER. THE TRAIL STARTS BETWEEN THOSE TWO DOGWOODS.

GOT IT, PADRE! LOOK ALIVE, 65!

THESE BOYS AREN'T JUST GOING TO LEARN TO SURVIVE, THEY ARE GOING TO LEARN TO LIVE. ARE YOU WITH ME OR NOT?

WHAT IF SOMETHING HAPPENS? I MEAN, I DON'T EVEN KNOW WHERE WE ARE.

THEY HAVE TO GROW UP SOONER OR LATER.

HEY LOOK, TRAVIS!

IT'S A STUPID FROG, MARVIN.

GUYS, IT SHOULD ONLY HAVE TAKEN AN HOUR AND FIFTEEN MINUTES TO GET TO CAMP BOBCAT.

BUT WE WERE DRIVING FOR--OH!

YOU GOTTA GET BETTER SHOES, PRABIR. YOU CAN'T WEAR THOSE ON HIKES.

I'M NOT GOOD AT... WALKING.

I HAVE TO TELL YOU BOYS SOMETHING. WE'RE NOT GOING TO CAMP BOBCAT.

WHAT DO YOU MEAN WE'RE NOT GOING TO CAMP BOBCAT? THAT DOESN'T MAKE ANY SENSE.

WHERE ARE WE GOING THEN?

JOHNNY CAN TALK?

ACTUALLY, I DON'T KNOW WHERE WE'RE GOING. I'M NOT EVEN SURE WHERE WE ARE NOW.

YOU DON'T EVEN KNOW? YOU'RE ASSISTANT TRIBE LEADER! WHAT'S WRONG WITH YOU?

TRAVIS, I'M AN ADULT, YOU CAN'T--

YOU'RE A WASTE, BUDDY.

IS THIS STILL AN OFFICIAL CAMPOUT? PATCHES CAN ONLY BE ISSUED AT OFFICIAL JUNIOR BRAVE ACTIVITIES.

AM I DOING THIS HIKE ALONE, TRIBE?

I'M SORRY PADRE, WE WERE JUST TAKING SOME TIME TO TALK ABOUT THE HIKE.

TRIBE LEADER SIR, WHY ARE WE NOT AT CAMP BOBCAT? ALSO, DO OUR PARENTS KNOW WHERE WE ARE?

WE ARE NOT GOING TO CAMP BOBCAT, BECAUSE CAMP BOBCAT IS FOR SISSIES. NOW, I WAS UNDER THE IMPRESSION THAT TRIBE 65 WAS, IN FACT, NOT SISSIES? AM I WRONG?

WELL, MAYBE--

WE'RE NO SISSIES, PADRE.

THERE ARE TWO KINDS OF EDIBLE MUSHROOMS NATIVE TO THIS PARTICULAR MOUNTAIN.

THAT'S NOT ONE OF THEM, AMIR.

PADRE, CAN WE TAKE A REST? I THINK PRABIR PASSED OUT.

I'M AWAKE, I JUST CAN'T FEEL MY LEGS.

CONGRATULATIONS BOYS, YOU SURVIVED. NOW LET'S MAKE CAMP.

YOU'RE SO SWEATY.

SHUT UP, MARVIN.

LIKE, HERE?

NOT HERE, TRAVIS.

JUST DO WHAT WE DID WHEN I WAS YOUR AGE--STRIP DOWN AND HOP IN NAKED.

IT'S VERY FREEING.

THAT'S CREEPY.

WHAT? WHAT'D I SAY?

IT'S A GENERATIONAL THING.

IF YOU DON'T HAVE TRUNKS, JUST JUMP IN IN YOUR UNDERWEAR OR SHORTS. YOUR CLOTHES WILL DRY.

BOMBS AWAY!

SPLOOSH

YOU APPRECIATE IT MORE IF YOU WORK FOR IT.

STILL COULD HAVE TOLD ME.

WORD GETS OUT ABOUT THIS PLACE...

THESE BOYS NEED TO SEE NATURE, UNFETTERED. A FAWN IN THE GLEN. A HAWK ON THE WING.

YOU KNOW, POETRY.

PT00

TRIBE LEADER PATTERSON, THIS PLACE IS REALLY COOL, WHAT'S IT CALLED?

WELL LUCAS, IT DOESN'T REALLY HAVE A NAME.

MOST THINGS IN THIS REGION WERE FIRST NAMED BY THE INDIANS, AND RIGHTLY SO MIND YOU. PERHAPS WE SHOULD LET AN INDIAN NAME THIS PLACE.

I THINK WE SHOULD CALL IT--

NOT YOU, PRABIR.

WHAT? SERIOUSLY?

...AND YOU MEAN "NATIVE AMERICAN."

BUT...

...NO.

DAY 4.

THERE WE GO. WE'RE GOING TO BE FIRST, MARVIN.

YES! I AM AWESOME!

GOOD JOB!

QUICK-START FIRE SKILLS PATCHES FOR YOU THREE. CONGRATULATIONS.

HEY JOHNNY, I KNOW THIS STUFF SEEMS KIND OF STUPID TO YOU.

'STUPID' ISN'T IT. JUST... POINTLESS.

SOME OF IT IS FUN, RIGHT?

FIZZLE

DAY 5.

SO, THIS FULFILLS MY CAMP COOK PATCH REQUIREMENTS. RIGHT, PADRE?

HAVEN'T SEEN THAT BEFORE.

AWESOME! LOOK AT THOSE JETS!

THOSE ARE BOEING B-52HS.

OH LIKE YOU KNOW.

NO, HE'S RIGHT. THOSE ARE HEAVY BOMBERS. MUST JUST BE ON PRACTICE FLIGHTS.

SEE, I KNOW STUFF. I SAW A SHOW ABOUT THEM ON THE HISTORY CHANNEL.

THEY NEVER FLY OVER THIS AREA THOUGH.

DAY 6.

THE SNARE ACTUALLY WORKED! IT NEVER WORKS IN CARTOONS.

IT PROBABLY DIED OF A HEART ATTACK WHEN THE TRAP SPRUNG.

MAKE A SMALL CUT ALONG THE LOWER BELLY. BE CAREFUL NOT TO PUNCTURE THE STOMACH LINING. THEN JUST SLOWLY PULL THE SKIN OFF.

I DON'T BELIEVE RABBIT SKINNING IS IN THE CURRENT EDITION OF THE HANDBOOK.

I DIDN'T LEARN IT FROM THE JUNIOR BRAVES.

HOLD YOUR HORSES, CHIEF.

YOU SERIOUSLY JUST CALLED ME 'CHIEF'?

...I CALL EVERYONE 'CHIEF.' I KNOW IT CAN'T BE EASY BEING IN YOUR SITUATION, WITH YOUR PARENTS--

PADRE, I'M TIRED OF PLAYING INDIANS WITH A BUNCH OF COWBOYS!

UM, HEY PADRE, WHAT ARE THESE STICKS FOR?

IT'S A TRAIL SIGN. YOU DON'T HAVE THAT PATCH YET, DO YOU? IT MEANS DANGER IS UP THAT TRAIL.

YOU WANT TO CHECK IT OUT?

NOT EVEN A LITTLE.

LEAVE ONLY FOOTPRINTS. TAKE ONLY MEMORIES.

DAY 7.

GREAT GREEN GOBS OF GREASY GRIMY GOPHER GUTS, MUTILATED MONKEY MEAT HAIRY PICKLED PIGGY FEET.

IT'S GOING TO SUCK GOING BACK TO SCHOOL TOMORROW.

JUST WAIT UNTIL YOU GET TO MIDDLE SCHOOL. I HATE THAT PLACE.

STOP RESTRICTED AREA

HEY PADRE, DO YOU THINK WE CAN GO BACK THIS SUMMER? PADRE?

BOYS, PUT YOUR HEADS--

TOO LATE.

36

BOYS, CALM DOWN. WE'LL STAY HERE TONIGHT AND FIGURE OUT WHERE EVERYONE WENT IN THE MORNING.

FORGET THAT! I'M GOING HOME. MARVIN, COME ON!

RUN HOME TO MOMMY, TRAVIS? YOU SPENT A WEEK AWAY AND YOU WERE FINE.

YOU ALL WERE FINE. ONE MORE NIGHT, ALL OF US TOGETHER IN A SAFE PLACE ISN'T GOING TO HURT ANYONE.

I WANT TO SEE MY MOM AND MY DAD SO BAD.

HEY PRABIR, IT WILL BE OKAY.

YOU DON'T KNOW!

PADRE, WHERE IS EVERYONE? 20,000 PEOPLE JUST DISAPPEARED.

LISTEN, SOMETHING HAPPENED. SOMETHING HORRIBLE. WE ARE LIVING FOR THESE BOYS NOW. YOU HEAR ME?

GRRARGH!

GRRARGH!

WHAT THE HELL WAS THAT?

SOUNDED LIKE AN ANIMAL OR SOMEONE WHO'S HURT.

DYLAN. SON GET AWAY FROM THE WINDOW.

TRAAAVIS.

SCRIK SCRIK

JUST BE QUIET, OKAY.

HEY GUYS, I TH--

CRASH

Keep Straight

Camp

Turn Right

Turn Left

Safe Place

Fire Pit

Be Careful

Danger

TRAIL MARKERS

A Junior Brave may find himself confronted with a strange path ahead. How will he know which way to proceed? If he's smart, he'll be observant for signs of those that came before him.

For centuries humans have used trail markers as a way to communicate to their fellow traveler. Some American Indians even shaped the very trees themselves into ancient "highway signs" pointing the path to villages or river crossings. Trail "blazes" are also a common form of marking. Although you may think "blaze" in this context refers to "fire," it actually means to cut a marker into the tree itself. Another method is the use of cairns, or pillars of rock, which can be used in areas without trees or plant growth. A favored form of trail marking by the Junior Braves is "posting," the planting of posts—or even simple sticks—in the ground to convey meaning.

On these pages you will find the most common symbols used in marking trails.

✕

CHAPTER TWO...

WHAT WAS I SUPPOSED TO DO? YOU ALL WERE JUST STANDING AROUND DOWN THERE LIKE A BUNCH OF MOUTH-BREATHERS!

YOU SAW WHAT HAPPENED!

NOW WE'RE UP HERE AND WE HAVE NOWHERE TO GO!

THEY'RE GOING TO TAKE US, JUST LIKE DYLAN!

THUMP

WE'LL CLIMB DOWN.

CLIMB DOWN! WITH THOSE... PEOPLE DOWN THERE!?!

UM.

THOSE ARE NOT PEOPLE!

FINE, YOU FIGURE IT OUT THEN, LUCAS!

46

MAYBE WE COULD USE THIS.

WELL, WE COULD... UM.

I DON'T KNOW WHAT TO DO! I'M JUST A KID!

WE'RE GOING TO ZIP-LINE DOWN TO THAT POLE AND THEN GET TO THE VAN AND DRIVE OUT OF HERE.

WHAT ARE YOU GOING TO DO? LASSO IT?

I'M NOT.

HE IS.

LAST YEAR, MRS. MATUCIE'S CLASS. YOU WROTE THAT ESSAY ABOUT WINNING THAT RODEO COMPETITION WITH YOUR DAD.

IT WAS WEIRD BECAUSE YOUR DAD SEEMS LIKE A WUSS.

THE RODEO WAS WITH MY REAL DAD, NOT HENRY. HENRY'S NOT A WUSS, HE TRIES.

ANYWAY, I ONLY TOOK THIRD.

WELL, NOW YOU REALLY NEED TO TAKE FIRST.

GIVE ME A SECOND.

HOW IS THIS GOING TO WORK?

TRAVIS. TRAVIS, LOOK!

SHUT UP, MARVIN.

GRUR!

AAHHHHH!

THAT DOOR WON'T HOLD-- HOLY!

WHAM!

SPLOSH

THAT'S DISGUSTING!

EWW!

WHOA. COOL.

WHAT WAS THAT THING?

GUYS! OH, GUYS!

WHACK

WHUMP

CRACK

GO!
NOW!

COME ON! HURRY GUYS!

I'M SCARED!

MARVIN, SERIOUSLY!

MARVIN, IT'S OKAY. WE'RE ALL SCARED, BUT WE HAVE TO DO THIS.

BOMBS AWAY!

WHUMP

I CAN'T--

--BELIEVE THAT ACTUALLY WORKED.

I LANDED IN SQUISH.

IT'S LOCKED!

THIS ONE IS TOO!

WHY DID PADRE LOCK IT? BUDDY, YOU HAVE KEYS RIGHT?

BUDDY! THE KEYS!

I DON'T HAVE THE KEYS.

BUDDY, WHAT'S ON YOUR LEG?

OH!

RUN!

DAMMIT!

AHHHH!

THIS WAY! COME ON!

I THINK WE LOST THEM.

WAIT.

EVERYONE BE QUIET.

MOM?

WHERE-- UGFF!

QUIET, MAN.

CAN WE TALK NOW?

YEAH.

ANYONE SEEN MY CAT?

CLICK

SHE'S NOT HERE.

I THOUGHT MY MOM WOULD BE HOME AND SHE'D TELL US WHAT'S GOING ON. WE SHOULD JUST SLEEP HERE. IT'S TOO DARK OUT.

IN THE MORNING WE CAN LOOK FOR OUR PARENTS. AND PADRE AND DYLAN.

TRAVIS IS RIGHT. LET'S GO UPSTAIRS AND GET SOME SLEEP IN ONE OF THE BEDROOMS.

I THINK WE SHOULD SLEEP IN THE BASEMENT. THERE'S MORE ROOM THERE THAN ANY OF THE BEDROOMS.

WHAT? THAT'S RIDICULOUS. WHAT IF THEY COME BACK? WE'D BE TRAPPED DOWN THERE. WE'LL SLEEP UPSTAIRS.

YEAH, BUT THEY MIGHT HEAR US FROM THE STREET OR SEE US MOVE PAST A WINDOW. IF THEY COME IN THE HOUSE, IT WILL BE OBVIOUS TO GO UPSTAIRS. WE'LL SLEEP IN THE BASEMENT.

YOU GUYS ARE RIDICULOUS.

FINE, WE'LL SPLIT UP. ANYONE WHO THINKS SLEEPING UPSTAIRS IS A BETTER IDEA, FOLLOW ME.

NO SLEEPING IN MY MOM'S BED. THAT'S GROSS.

YOU STICKING WITH ME, AMIR?

NO. YOUR BIG BUTT IS JUST BLOCKING THE STAIRS. MOVE IT.

JERK. I GUESS NONE OF YOU SAW "NIGHT OF THE LIVING DEAD."

I WANT TO SLEEP IN MY ROOM. I WANT MY PILLOW.

BASEMENT, MARVIN.

AWWW, MAN.

HERE'S WHAT I THINK HAPPENED-- OKAY, TERRORISTS SMUGGLED A BOMB INTO ROSELAND, AND WERE HOLDING THE TOWN HOSTAGE.

WHY WOULD THEY DO THAT?

WHY WOULDN'T THEY DO THAT? THEY'RE TERRORISTS!

SO THOSE THINGS ARE TERRORISTS?

NO. THE BOMB WENT OFF AND IT MUTATED PEOPLE. THEY STARTED EATING EACH OTHER'S FACES AND ≷YAWN≷ SETTING DOGS ON FIRE.

HEY, REMEMBER WHEN OUR COUSIN GOT STUNG BY A BEE LAST SUMMER? HIS FACE GOT ALL SWELLED UP. MAYBE REALLY BIG BEES STUNG EVERYONE AND THEY JUST HAVE TO TAKE SOME MEDICINE AND THEY'LL GET BETTER.

MARVIN, THAT'S STUPID. THAT'S SO STUPID. DON'T TALK ANYMORE. GO TO SLEEP.

WHATEVER TRAVIS. I'M SO TELLING... MOM... ZZZ.

DON'T WORRY. TOMORROW, WE'LL FIND EVERYONE'S PARENTS.

IS ANYONE ELSE COLD? THIS HOUSE IS DRAFTY.

I THINK I HEARD SOMEONE DOWNST--

MEOWWAAH!

WAS THAT A CAT?

SSSSH. IT CAME FROM OUTSIDE.

HSSSS

IT'S... NOTHING. JUST TRY TO GO TO SLEEP.

SCRIK SCRIK SCRIK

ANYONE ELSE HEAR THAT?

GUYS, I TOLD YOU I HEARD SOMETHING DOWNSTAIRS.

JUST TRY TO SLEEP, OKAY?

JUST TRY.

DAY 8.

HEY, MARVIN?

WHAT THE HELL?

GUYS, DON'T EAT SO FAST. AT LEAST TASTE THE FOOD.

PEANUT BUTTER COMES IN 'CHUNKY?' WE DON'T HAVE THIS AT HOME.

THE FRIDGE ISN'T WORKING. DON'T DRINK THE MILK.

THAT'S OUR FOOD! YOU CAN'T TAKE OUR FOOD! GET YOUR OWN!

USUALLY THE BIG CITY IS NOT WHERE YOU WANT TO BE IN A CRISIS.

THE ELECTRICITY IS OUT SO THE RADIOS AND T.V.S AREN'T WORKING AND THOSE USUALLY TELL YOU WHAT TO DO.

BACK HOME WE HAD A BLIZZARD AND THEY SET UP EMERGENCY SHELTERS; SCHOOLS, CHURCHES, FIRE STATIONS.

I THINK THE CHURCH IS OUT.

I HAVE TO GO NUMBER ONE,

IS YOUR BATHROOM THIS WAY?

OH. WOW. TRAVIS...

WHAT?

YOU NEED TO COME HERE.

OH MAN! SOME JERKFACE STOLE MY T.V. AND 360!

MARVIN, WE'VE BEEN ROBBED BY A JERKFACE!

THAT'S THE LEAST OF YOUR WORRIES.

OH, BALLZ!

OHHH, THAT'S WHY IT WAS DRAFTY.

OUR HOUSE.

MOM'S GOING TO BE MAD.

SHUT UP, MARVIN.

THE HOUSE ISN'T SAFE. TRAVIS, GET ANY MEDICINE OR FIRST AID SUPPLIES. LUCAS, GET THE FOOD TOGETHER. JOHNNY, CAN YOU GET--

JOHNNY'S NOT HERE.

WHAT DO YOU MEAN? HE'S RIGHT--

HE'S NOT HERE.

THEY TOOK HIM!

NO, HE LEFT WHILE YOU GUYS WERE SLEEPING.

MARVIN, JUST BECAUSE THE HOUSE IS TRASHED DOESN'T MEAN YOU CAN DRAW ON THE DOOR.

ALSO, WHY ARE YOU DRAWING ON THE DOOR?

I CAN'T BELIEVE WE LOST ANOTHER ONE.

WHY WOULD HE LEAVE?

THAT MEANS WE HAVE TO FIND DYLAN, PADRE, OUR PARENTS AND JOHNNY!

SCRIK SCRIK

WAIT. THE BAG.

SCRIK SCRIK

SCRIK
SCRIK

GET YOUR GEAR. WE'RE GOING NOW. WE'LL FIND ONE OF THOSE EMERGENCY SHELTERS.

SCRIK SCRIK SCREEEE

LET'S JUST HOPE JOHNNY FINDS HIS WAY.

HOW TO MAKE A PB&J SANDWICH

FT PRASHIR AND MARVIN

U WILL NEED:

BREAD!

P B.!

J!

STEP 1!

THE SECRET IS TO MAKE THE PEANUT BUTTER THICKEST AT THE FOUR EDGES OF THE BREAD.

PB!

STEP 2!

MAKE THE JELLY
THICKEST IN THE
MIDDLE OF THE
BREAD.

J!

STEP 3!

WHEN YOU PUT
THE TWO PIECES
OF BREAD TOGETHER
THE THICK PEANUT
BUTTER EDGES
HELP SEAL IN THE
JELLY!

SLAP!

THAT WAY IT DOESN'T
SQUIRT OUT AND GET
OVER YOUR UNIFORM
OR HANDS!

I HATE HAVING
MESSY HANDS!

TRAVIS DA
STERK!

CHAPTER THREE...

MR. BAKER?
IS THAT YOU?
MR. BAKER?

TOSS

OH MAN, MR. BAKER, IS THAT YOU? IT'S JOHNNY. REMEMBER ME? YOU USED TO HELP ME CROSS THE STREET.

AHHH!

HEY! HEY! HELP!

VROOM

STOP!

JOHNNY REDCLAY? FOURTH PERIOD EARTH SCIENCE! OH MY GOD! JOHNNY, GET IN! HURRY!

MR. MIKISHKA? WHAT'S HAPPENING?

WHAT ARE YOU DOING OUT BY YOURSELF? I THOUGHT YOU WERE ONE OF THE INFECTED. WE'LL GET YOU BACK TO THE SCHOOL AND EVERYTHING WILL BE FINE!

MY JUNIOR BRAVE TRIBE WAS ON A CAMPING TRIP FOR A WEEK, WE GOT BACK LAST NIGHT. EVERYONE ELSE IS--

TOTALLY FINE. TOTALLY FINE.

...WELL UM, I'M NOT SURE WHERE THEY ARE.

EWW.

WHY CAN'T WE BE LUCKY ENOUGH TO FIND AN UNLOCKED CAR WITH THE KEYS INSIDE?

IT SMELLS LIKE FEET.

CHURCH IS WRECKED, SOMEONE BURNED DOWN THE FIRE STATION--IRONY. THE NEXT POSSIBILITY IS THE SCHOOL.

WE HAVEN'T SEEN ANY ZOMBIES SINCE TRAVIS AND MARVIN'S HOUSE. MAYBE THEY ARE NOCTURNAL?

GUYS! I FOUND SOMETHING!

IT'S JOHNNY'S HAT.

SO?

I'VE NEVER SEEN JOHNNY WITHOUT HIS HAT.

ME EITHER.

I REPEAT-- SO? THE DUDE LEFT US. HE CAN FEND FOR HIMSELF.

BUT, THE MUTANT WAS RUN OVER. YOU CAN SEE THE TIRE TRACKS.

A TIRE MEANS A CAR AND A CAR MEANS A PERSON DRIVING IT. AND A PERSON MEANS PEOPLE.

UM, YEAH. GOOD THINKING, DORKUS.

THE CAR MADE A TRAIL OF MUTANT GOO ALL DOWN THE STREET.

MAYBE JOHNNY GOT IN THE CAR.

STRANGER DANGER.

ENJOY SPRING BREAK

HONK

IS THAT THE LUNCH LADY?

79

PROBABLY THE FIRST TIME YOU'RE HAPPY ABOUT GOING TO THE PRINCIPAL'S OFFICE, RIGHT?

WHERE IS EVERYONE? I THOUGHT YOU SAID EVERYONE WAS HERE.

MIKISHKA! WHERE WERE YOU?

OH MY. OH MY MY. A STUDENT! A LIVE STUDENT!

WHERE IS EVERYONE ELSE? WHERE'S THE OTHER KIDS? THE PARENTS?

IT'S OKAY. YOU'RE JOHNNY, RIGHT? I REMEMBER YOU. HELP WILL BE HERE SOON. IN THE MEANTIME, WE NEED TO STICK TO A SCHEDULE. IT'S ALMOST EIGHT O'CLOCK!

I'M GOING TO TAKE THE CAR OUT AND TRY TO FIND HIS FRIENDS.

THERE'S MORE STUDENTS? HUZZAH!

COME ON, SQUIRT.

SORRY I'M LATE.

NOW, NORMALLY MR. NOLAND WOULD BE TEACHING THIS CLASS, BUT HE'S DEAD.

I'LL BE TAKING OVER UNTIL WE CAN FILL THAT VACANCY.

MRS. GARVEY, IT'S LIKE WORLD WAR THREE HAPPENED.

WHAT ARE THOSE THINGS OUT THERE? THE ONE MR. MIKISHKA RAN OVER, I'M PRETTY SURE WAS THE CROSSING GUARD.

SHHH. SHHH. THIS IS A HISTORY CLASS, NOT CURRENT EVENTS. LET'S LEARN, SHALL WE? "SECTION 5; MANIFEST DESTINY." THIS WAS ONE OF MY FAVORITE SUBJECTS WHEN I WAS IN SCHOOL. "DURING THE 1830S AND 1840S"--

THIS IS POINTLESS. THERE'S NOBODY HERE. WHERE DID EVERYBODY GO?

GET BACK TO YOUR SEAT YOU UNGRATEFUL BRAT! YOU GET UP AGAIN AND I'LL THROW YOU OUTSIDE AND LET THOSE MONSTERS HAVE THEIR WAY WITH YOU!

AHEM.

I APOLOGIZE. LET US CONTINUE.

MAY I SHARPEN A PENCIL SO I CAN TAKE NOTES?

OH. SURE. GO AHEAD. I WILL CONTINUE READING, SO PLEASE STILL PAY ATTENTION.

"--THAT THE GREAT NATION SHOULD SPREAD FROM THE ATLANTIC TO THE PACIFIC, UNBROKEN. A BEACON OF FREEDOM AND CIVILIZATION FOR EVEN THE UNENLIGHTENED AND INDIGENOUS PEOPLES OF THE CONTINENT."

THAT'S PRETTY NEAT, HUH? INSPIRING.

JOHNNY, WHY DON'T YOU READ THE NEXT SECTION ALOUD TO THE CLASS?

I HATE THIS PLACE.

THE GOO TRAIL LED HERE. MAYBE LUCAS WAS RIGHT AND THEY TURNED THE SCHOOL INTO AN EMERGENCY SHELTER.

DOES THIS PLACE LOOK LIKE A SAFE HAVEN TO ANYONE?

LOOK, UP IN THE WINDOW.

WHAT ARE THOSE? PENCILS?

IT'S A TRAIL SIGN. IT'S IN THE GUIDEBOOK, TRAVIS. DUUHH.

SHUT YOUR MOUTH OR I'M GOING TO PUNCH OUT YOUR TEETH AND THEN MOM IS GOING TO BE SO MAD AT YOU FOR HAVING NO TEETH.

NO, HE'S RIGHT. IT'S A SIGN.

YEAH. I GOT THAT PATCH A WHILE BACK. I FORGET WHAT THAT TRAIL SIGN MEANS THOUGH.

IT MEANS DANGER.

YOU GUYS STAY HERE.

OH, HI. I'M BUDDY LANDON. I WENT TO THIS SCHOOL ABOUT TWELVE YEARS AGO. I USED TO ASK FOR EXTRA MAC AND CHEESE?

AHH!

SHAKE
SHAKE
SHAKE

CRACK

I THINK HE'S DEAD.

HE'S NOT--

YEAH, HE MIGHT BE DEAD.

THIS WON'T DO.

YOU THINK JUST BECAUSE WE ARE LIVING IN EXTRAORDINARY TIMES THAT YOU CAN SKIP CLASS. OH NO-NO!

I WASN'T SKIPPING CLASS, BECAUSE THERE ISN'T ANY CLASS TO SKIP.

I WILL MAKE AN EXAMPLE OUT OF YOU BECAUSE YOU HAVE FAILED TO BE AN EXAMPLE TO THE OTHER STUDENTS!

WHAT? WHAT OTHER--

I WANT YOU TO THINK ABOUT THE GRAVITY OF YOUR ACTIONS. YOU ARE A STUDENT AT SACAJAWEA MIDDLE SCHOOL. YOU SHOULD TAKE PRIDE IN THAT.

YOU KNOW, CULTURALLY.

NO USE.

THANK YOU! THANK YOU SO MUCH, MA'AM.

JUST DON'T TELL MRS. GARVEY ABOUT THE PIZZA.

LUNCH TIME.

DISGUSTING.

THIS IS ALL JUST TEMPORARY ANYWAY. HELP WILL ARRIVE IN NO TIME.

THIS IS REALLY THE LAST OF THE MEAT?

OH, I THINK I CAN STRETCH OUR SUPPLY OUT JUST A BIT LONGER.

TIME FOR FIFTH PERIOD BIOLOGY.

ERRRNGH!

OOOF!

GET HIM OVER HERE.

GIVE IT UP, SQUIRT!

LET GO!

CALM DOWN. THIS IS IMPORTANT, SO LISTEN UP.

EVERYONE THOUGHT WE WERE CRAZY FOR STAYING, BUT I KNEW--I KNEW!-- WHAT WAS GOING ON. IT'S A VIRUS! THAT'S THE ONLY EXPLANATION.

THIS WAS ALL CAUSED BY A VIRUS? WHAT KIND OF SICKNESS MAKES PEOPLE'S BODIES LOOK LIKE THAT?

WE WERE ONLY GONE A WEEK, HOW DID THIS ALL HAPPEN? WHAT VIRUS CAN TAKE OVER EVERYONE THAT FAST?

OH, I DON'T KNOW--MAYBE SICKNESS BRED OUT OF WORLDWIDE CALAMITY, FOR STARTERS!

I HAVE NO IDEA WHAT THEY'LL CALL THE VIRUS, BUT I KNOW WHAT THEY'LL CALL THE CURE!

MIKISHKALUM!

OR MIKISHKAFLAN. I HAVEN'T DECIDED.

YOU'RE GOING TO TRY TO CURE THIS DISEASE? YOU'RE A SIXTH GRADE SCIENCE TEACHER.

DUDE, COME ON.

I'M THE SMARTEST MAN IN THIS WHOLE DAMNED TOWN! AND ONCE I CURE THE INFECTION AND SAVE SOCIETY, EVERYONE WILL KNOW!

I FINALLY HAVE WHAT I NEEDED--A FRESH SPECIMEN. ONLY A FEW MORE TESTS TO DO AND THEN WE'LL BE DONE.

I'M SORRY TO DO THIS, JOHNNY. I NEED TO WATCH THE EFFECTS UP CLOSE.

RRRRGHN!

YOU'RE A REAL HERO.

DID YOU GET THAT FROM MY INSULIN BAG? 'KISH, I NEED THOSE!

THIS IS SCIENCE!

FIRST, WE DRAW A SAMPLE FROM SUBJECT NUMBER ONE.

SECOND, WE STERILIZE THE NEEDLE.

THIRD, WE INJECT THE SAMPLE INTO SUBJECT NUMBER TWO.

HURRY IT UP. I THINK I HEAR GARVEY COMING.

I WANT YOU TO KNOW THAT I WILL HAPPILY TELL THE STORY OF THAT BRAVE LITTLE INDIAN BOY WHO GAVE HIS LIFE TO CURE THE WORLD.

GET AWAY FROM ME!

IT'S THE ONLY WAY!

CRAK

WAS THAT A BASEBALL?

CRAK

I SEE TWO ADULTS. THEY LOOK REALLY MAD. MAYBE WE SHOULDN'T BE BREAKING THESE WINDOWS?

YOU KIDS STAY RIGHT THERE!

GUYS! GET OUT OF HERE! THEY'RE CRAZY!

I MIGHT NEED THOSE KIDS! EVEN IF IT'S JUST TO GIVE GARVEY SOMETHING TO DO SO SHE STAYS OUT OF OUR WAY.

THAT KID WITH THE BAT HAS A KILLER SWING! CAN YOU NOT INFECT HIM? WE'LL NEED HIM COME BASEBALL SEASON.

LEAVE HIM ALONE, JERKFACE!

KRAV MAGA!

IT SMELLS HERE.

CABBAGE. I LIKE CABBAGE.

YOU'RE WEIRD, MARVIN. I STILL SAY--

SSSH! I THINK THEY LIKE GARBAGE.

WHERE DID THEY GO? I TOLD THEM TO STAY PUT. STUPID KIDS NEVER LISTEN.

UGGH, THEY'RE SO DISGUSTING.

THANKS FOR COMING TO SAVE ME.

IT WAS PRETTY STUPID ≈HUFF≈ GOING OFF LIKE THAT. ≈HUFF≈ REAL STUPID!

I DIDN'T THINK YOU GUYS WOULD.

JOHNNY, I WANT YOU TO KNOW SOMETHING...

...AMIR DIDN'T EVEN WANT TO COME SAVE YOU. THIS WAS ALL ME.

WHAT!?

WHOA! DON'T GO KUNG-JEW ON ME! I WAS JUST KIDDING!

WE SHOULD PROBABLY GET MOVING.

WHERE ARE THEY KEEPING BUDDY?

WHAT DO YOU MEAN?

YOU HAVEN'T SEEN HIM? THE LUNCH LADY HIT HIM OVER THE HEAD AND DRAGGED HIM INSIDE.

NO WAY. MAYBELLE'S NICE. SHE GAVE ME A PIZZA AND CANDY BARS FOR LUNCH.

MAYBELLE? YOU KNOW HER NAME? SHE'S A WHACKJOB. SHE ATE A CAT--A LIVE CAT!

THROUGH THE CAFETERIA, IT'S A SHORTCUT.

WHOA.

I WOULD HAVE TRIED TO CURE YOU! I SWEAR!

WHO SHOULD WE HELP?

OURSELVES.

CAN WE GO? IT'S GETTING HARD TO BREATHE.

I ALWAYS KNEW THERE WAS SOMETHING WRONG WITH THIS SCHOOL.

♪ TWEET ♪

♪ TWEET / TWEET ♪

YOU GUYS SET THE SCHOOL ON FIRE?

YOU GUYS ARE GOING TO GET IN TROUBLE WHEN THIS IS ALL OVER.

THIS ISN'T GOING TO BE OVER ANYTIME SOON. MR. MIKISHKA SAID IT WAS A VIRUS THAT WAS MAKING PEOPLE TURN INTO MONSTERS. IT SOUNDED LIKE THE WHOLE WORLD WAS SICK.

HE WAS ALSO CRAZY. SO THERE'S THAT.

WE NEED TO GET OFF THE STREETS. THAT SMOKE IS GOING TO ATTRACT A LOT OF ATTENTION.

THE BLACKFOOT STORY OF TWO BEARS

One evening an old Blackfoot told his grandson about a battle that goes on inside people.

He said, "My son, the battle is between two bears inside us all.

"One is Evil—It is anger, envy, jealousy, sorrow, regret, greed, arrogance, self-pity, guilt, resentment, inferiority, lies, false pride, superiority, and ego.

"The other is Good—It is joy, peace, love, hope, serenity, humility, kindness, benevolence, empathy, generosity, truth, compassion and faith."

The grandson thought about it for a minute and then asked his grandfather: "Which bear wins?"

The Blackfoot replied, "The one you feed."

×

EVERYONE KNOWS "DON'T FEED THE BEARS." DUH.
—MARVIN

GUYS, THIS STORY IS A BOGUS WHITE PEOPLE THING! I MEAN COME ON!
—JOHNNY

CHAPTER FOUR...

KIDS? WHAT THE HELL ARE KIDS DOING HERE?

IT'S A POLICEMAN! HE LOOKS NORMAL-- I MEAN NOT LIKE A MONSTER.

THAT'S NOT A POLICEMAN.

HOLD UP! HOLD UP!

I SAID-- HOLD UP!

CHECK IT OUT DUDES, PRETTY COOL, HUH? THE STORE IS OURS.

LOOK WHAT I FOUND! JUNIOR BRAVES!

IF OUR FAMILIES AREN'T HERE, THAT MEANS THEY GOT EVACUATED, RIGHT? SO THEY'RE SAFE. OR MAYBE THEY'RE HERE.

YOU SHOULD HAVE SEEN THIS PLACE A COUPLE OF DAYS AGO, MAN. IT WAS A ZOO!

SEGEL
KRAV M

SEGEEKM@G

EXIT

PEOPLE GRABBING EVERYTHING! NOT USEFUL STUFF EITHER, LIKE BATTERIES OR CIGARETTES.

77

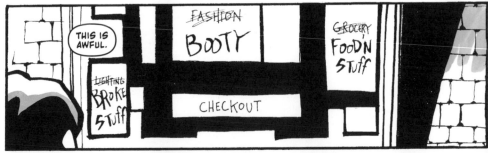

THIS IS AWFUL.

~~FASHION~~ BOOTY

~~LIGHTING~~ BROKE STUFF

~~GROCERY~~ FOOD'N STUFF

CHECKOUT

EVERYONE HERE IS IN A UNIFORM.

KEITH, WHERE ARE THE REGULAR PEOPLE?

CAMPR

THERE WERE SOME CITIZENS, BUT I THINK THEY ALL KINDA LEFT AFTER A FEW DAYS.

I GUESS THEY DIDN'T LIKE IT HERE.

BILL'S MY SUPERVISOR, HE'S REALLY AWESOME, MAN.

WHERE'D YOU FIND THE GETALONG GANG?

AT THE MIDDLE SCHOOL. THEY MISSED THE WHOLE THING MAN. THEY WERE ON A JUNIOR BRAVES CAMPING TRIP.

...

THEY CAN BED DOWN IN 7A. I DON'T THINK ANYONE'S STAKED OUT THAT AISLE YET. PILLOWS ARE IN 3B.

THERE'S NO PARENTS HERE, ARE THERE?

WHO NEEDS PARENTS, KID?

HOLD UP, TUBS. YOU LOOK FAMILIAR.

I SHOPLIFTED CANDY BARS AT THE SACK & SAVE YOU USED TO WORK AT. YOU NEVER CAUGHT ME THOUGH.

I'M TELLING MOM YOU'RE A STEALER!

SHUT UP, MARVIN.

I LIKE THAT FAT KID, BUT WHO'S THE DUDE? AN OLDER BROTHER?

HE'S ASSISTANT TRIBE WHATEVER.

HAVE TROY AND SHORT STEVE TAKE HIM OUT ON A SUPPLY RUN IN THE MORNING.

I KNOW YOU TOOK THE LAST CASE OF PABST! THAT WAS MINE!

I DIDN'T TAKE NO CASE OF PABST! I DRINK HEINEKEN! YOU SON OF--

HEY! THERE'S KIDS HERE!

THERE ARE KIDS HERE. DANG, THAT'S WEIRD.

I BET SHORT STEVE TOOK IT.

PROBABLY. THAT LITTLE PIGFACE IS A TOOL.

REDNECKS.

WHAT'S HEINEKEN?

PORK CHOPS.

SHUT UP, MARVIN.

WHAT? WHAT ABOUT PORK CHOPS?

ARE THEY GOOD? THEY LOOK GOOD IN PICTURES.

MONDAY NIGHT IS PORK CHOP NIGHT.

SPAGHETTI NIGHT.

KHICHDI NIGHT.

MY MOM DOESN'T COOK.

MEGHAN MAKES THIS THING WITH LENTILS, BUT SHE'S NOT... MY MOM... NEVERMIND.

WORK IT OUT AMONGST YOURSELVES, BUT SOMEONE'S GOING TO CLEAN THE CRAPPER AND SOMEONE'S GOING TO TAKE CARE OF THAT PILE OF GARBAGE BY THE CHECKOUTS.

DIBS ON GARBAGE.

DIBS ON NOTHING, MARVIN.

WHY ARE WE GOING TO DO ANY OF THIS? YOU'VE GOT TWENTY RENT-A-COP LUGS SITTING AROUND.

THINK OF IT THIS WAY, KID--MOMMY AND DADDY GIVE YOU CHORES, RIGHT? THESE ARE YOUR NEW CHORES.

WE GET AN ALLOWANCE FOR DOING CHORES. YOU GOING TO PAY US? IF NOT-- NO DEAL.

HOUSEWARES

IF YOU MAKE US, WE'RE JUST GOING TO DO A CRAPPY JOB AND WHINE A LOT, AND THAT'S GOING TO ANNOY ALL OF YOUR DUDES.

TELL YOU WHAT, YOU GUYS DO A GOOD JOB, TOMORROW WE'LL HELP YOU FIND YOUR MOMMIES.

WHAT DO YOU SAY, BIG GUY?

FINE.
DEAL.

THERE
YOU GO,
JOHNNY.

GLAD
WE WORKED
THAT OUT. I WAS
WORRIED FOR
A MOMENT.
HEH.

I THOUGHT THAT BILL GUY SAID TO TAKE THE TRASH OUT THE BACK.

DID HE? I DIDN'T HEAR THAT.

YOU WERE RIGHT THERE, TRAVIS.

SLAM

WAS I?

HEY, I DON'T THINK IT'S SAFE FOR US TO BE CARRYING THESE BAGS OUTSIDE. I THINK THE MUTANTS LIKE GARBAGE.

WHAT DID YOU SAY ABOUT THE GARBAGE?

I THINK THE MUTANTS ARE ATTRACTED TO GARBAGE. TRAVIS, WE SHOULD GO BACK INSIDE.

WELL, LET'S SEE IF THEY ARE.

AH!

HEY BRAVES, YOU'RE NOT SUPPOSED TO BE OUT HERE.

IT'S DANGEROUS.

AW MAN, COME ON, KEITH.

LET'S GO BACK INSIDE. THERE'S DEGENERATE DRUNKS AND IT COULD RAIN AND THERE'S THOSE THINGS WANDERING AROUND.

...BUT THERE MIGHT BE THOSE THINGS WANDERING AROUND.

BRAH, IT'S DAYTIME. IF YOU HAD SKIN LIKE THEIRS, WOULD YOU WANDER AROUND IN THE SUN?

ONLY THE REALLY FAR GONE ONES GO OUT INTO THE LIGHT.

JUST GO INSIDE AND SEE IF ANYONE IS THERE. IF THERE IS, JUST SCREAM, Y'KNOW.

EARN YOUR KEEP!

THIS IS CRAZY.

WE CAN MOVE TO THE NEXT ONE, THERE'S NO ONE THERE.

YOU STAY HERE, WE'LL BE BACK.

BUT THERE'S NO ONE--

YOU'RE STEALING FROM PEOPLE.

THAT'S LIKE, ONE WAY TO LOOK AT IT.

THE OTHER WAY IS TO SAY THAT WE ARE PRESERVING HISTORY.

I'M NOT DOING THIS. I NEED TO FIND OUT WHAT HAPPENED.

I KNOW WHAT'S GONNA HAPPEN IF YOU DON'T GET WITH THE PROGRAM--I TAZE YOU AND LEAVE YOU HERE.

AND THEN YOU GET YOUR THROAT RIPPED OUT BY A DOZEN SICKOS WITH EFFED-UP FACES.

SUN UP TOMORROW, WE'LL BRING YOUR LITTLE BRAVES OUT HERE AND HAVE THEM DO SOME REAL WORK.

POOR BABY, NOT USED TO DOING REAL WORK, ARE YOU?

THIS IS SUCH CRAP. I'M GOING BACK TO THE CAMP.

How to Dress a Wound

First, survey the area.

Check for whatever caused the wound, and make sure you and the victim are safe.

Next, assess the damage.
Ask what happened,
and offer to help.

If bleeding severely, elevate the wound and apply gentle pressure to both it and the nearest artery.

You can also get the victim to do this.

If the wound is severe call 911.
Use your best judgement—if in doubt, call.

HA, YEAH RIGHT,
BECAUSE 911 IS STILL
A THING.
—Johnny

Be sure to talk to the victim while you treat them. It can keep them calm, and also keep them from passing out due to shock or blood loss.

Rinse the wound with clean water, for about five minutes if practical. Clean with antibiotic cream or iodine.

YOU CAN ALSO USE SUGAR! (THANKS LUCAS!) PRABR

Bandage the wound lightly with gauze or cloth. The wrapping should be firm, but not constrict blood flow.

Keep the victim hydrated and monitor them for signs of shock.

If there is an ambulance coming, wait for it. If not, wait until the victim feels well enough to move, and take them to the nearest hospital for emergency care.

CHAPTER FIVE...

IF I TOLD HER ONCE, I TOLD HER A HUNDRED TIMES, IF IT WERE BETWEEN HER AND THE TRUCK, I'D TAKE THE TRUCK.

SO WHAT DOES SHE DO WHEN EVAC COMES? DUMB BROAD TAKES THE TRUCK AND HEADS EAST.

I HOPE SHE LOOKS IN THE GLOVE BOX BECAUSE YOU KNOW WHAT SHE'LL FIND?

HER SISTER'S PANTIES.

HEH.

HI!

WHAT THE HELL?

YOU'RE SMART. CAN YOU FIX IT?

WELL... HMMM.

A RADIO! WE JUST NEEDED A RADIO.

WHEN PEOPLE LOOTED THE STORE, I THINK THEY TOOK THE EASY TO CARRY MODELS.

WHOEVER PUT THIS TOGETHER HAD NO IDEA HOW TO DO ANYTHING.

GIVE ME A FEW MINUTES.

SOOOO, WHAT ARE YOU GUYS DOING?

MY FRIENDS AND I ARE PLAYING 'GO FISH'. WANNA JOIN IN?

GUYS! CURTIS GOT BIT ON HIS RUN.

HE'S BLEEDING REAL BAD.

BRING A MOP, KID.

147

DANG, I THINK IT LEFT SOME TEETH IN THERE.

DON'T YOU GUYS KNOW THE FIRST THING ABOUT FIRST AID? HE'S GOING TO LOSE THAT LEG.

JOHNNY, CAN YOU FIND ME SOME HYDROGEN PEROXIDE OR SUGAR? PRABIR, GRAB ME WATER.

SUGAR?

THIS KID DOESN'T KNOW WHAT HE'S DOING!

THIS MEDIC PATCH SAYS THAT I DO!

BACTERIA CAN'T GROW ON SUGAR. IN A PINCH IT WORKS PRETTY WELL TO TREAT A WOUND.

WHERE'S MY BROTHER?

MARVIN? YO! STINK FACE, YOU IN HERE? HEY, WHAT'S THIS?

COME ON YOU PIECE OF JUNK!

WHRR!

HAH! I SHOWED YOU!

BEEP BEEP BA-BEEP

THAT'S MORSE CODE. CRAP, I DON'T REMEMBER THAT STUFF! WHAT DOES THAT 'BEEP BEEP' MEAN?

I KNOW WHAT IT MEANS. IT MEANS GAME ON, MAN!

BRICKSTONE

THIS IS SOOO COOL! IT'S EPIC!

I FIXED THE GENERATOR!

I'M A GENIUS!

VIDEO GAMES? WE WERE GOING TO USE THAT!

YOU CAN USE IT WHEN WE'RE DONE.

WE'RE JUST GONNA PLAY FOR A LITTLE BIT.

THREE HOURS LATER.

DID YOU SEE THAT!

THAT WAS SO AWESOME.

IT WAS KIND OF QUIET OUT THERE.

TELL THAT TO CURTIS. EVERYONE IN YOUR CAR CAME BACK SAFELY. WE'LL SEE WHAT HAPPENS TOMORROW.

LOOK WHAT THAT FAT KID DID. HE FIXED THE GENERATOR.

ARE YOU GUYS CRAZY? YOU CAN'T RUN A GAS GENERATOR INSIDE! WE'RE GOING TO DIE OF CARBON MONOXIDE POISONING.

IT'S A BIG STORE, IT WOULD TAKE A REALLY LONG TIME FOR IT TO GET TO 'KILL US' LEVELS. KEEP COOL, BUDDY.

YEAH, KEEP COOL, BUDDY.

YOU GUYS HAVE A WORKING GENERATOR AND THIS IS HOW YOU GUYS USE IT? THAT THING'S A TOOL, BILL.

A POWERFUL TOOL.

GET YOUR ASS BACK TO THE TOY SECTION WITH THE OTHER BRATS.

GET SOME LAMPS FROM HOUSEWARES AND PUT OUT THE BARREL FIRES. THIS PLACE DOESN'T HAVE TO SMELL LIKE BURNING GARBAGE.

ALSO, ARE THE BEERS COLD YET?

GRRRRR!

PSY

WHOOP WHOOOP BUR BUR WHOOOO

PERIMETER BREACH!

RIGHT SIDE! RIGHT SIDE!

WOK

BATTER UP, BRAH!

DIG A HOLE FOR THAT ONE, HE'S DONE!

BUY KO

PRETTY COOL HUH? THE CAR ALARMS WERE BILL'S IDEA. WE ALWAYS KNOW WHEN THEY ARE COMING.

YEAH, PRETTY COOL, KEITH.

153

DAY 10.

I NEVER THOUGHT I'D CRAVE AN APPLE SO BAD IN MY LIFE.

I CAN'T EAT ANY OF THIS.

CAN'T OR WON'T?

HELPING YOURSELF TO THE KITCHEN I SEE.

YOU'RE HELPING US FIND OUR PARENTS TODAY, RIGHT?

THAT'S WHAT YOU SAID, REMEMBER?

DID I? THAT DOES SOUND KIND OF FAMILIAR.

I CAN HELP YOU BOYS, BUT I NEED YOU TO DO SOMETHING ELSE FOR US. YOU DID SUCH A GOOD JOB YESTERDAY...

...I'M PUTTING YOU IN CHARGE OF OUR NEXT BEAUTIFICATION PROJECT.

WHAT ARE WE DIGGING?

WHAT DO YOU THINK? THERE'S A LOT OF BODIES AROUND, PRABIR.

OH.

JUST GIVE A YELL IF YOU NEED A HAND.

YEAH. I'LL BE SURE TO DO THAT.

CREAK

TROY! STEVE! I NEED HELP!

I SAID I NEED HELP!

I HOPE YOU WERE RIGHT, TRAVIS.

WHUMP WHUMP WHUMP

UNNGH.

SKLSH!

UGLY PIECE OF--!

THERE HE IS!

GUYS, HELP ME!

SLOW DOWN, TROY.

STEVE, I SWEAR I'M GOING TO-- UNGH!

TROY! YOU'RE A DECENT GUY! HELP ME!

BRAH, THAT'S SWEET.

AWW, HOW'D YOU GET SO GOOD?

I'M A GAMING GOD!

WHRRR

HEY, WHAT ARE YOU GUYS DOING?

WE'RE WORKING, TRAVIS. WHAT ARE YOU DOING?

I--I CAN HELP YOU GUYS.

NAH, NAH DUDE. THEY GOT IT. STICK AROUND, LET'S LEVEL UP.

WHAT DO YOU WANT TO DIG A LATRINE FOR? STICK AROUND. CARROT TOP AND SITTING BULL GOT IT. DON'T YOU GUYS?

YEAH. WE GOT IT. YOU'RE WORKING JUST AS HARD, RIGHT?

FINE, YOU GUYS HAVE FUN WITH THAT!

ROUND'S STARTING, DUDE.

HEY KEITH, WHERE DO YOU THINK OUR PARENTS WENT?

OH MAN, I HAVE NO CLUE. THE BUSES HEADED WEST, BUT I HEARD THAT'S WHERE THINGS WERE THE CRAZIEST.

TELL THE TRUTH, I WAS REALLY DRUNK WHEN ALL THAT WENT DOWN.

SIP?

I GOTTA USE THE BATHROOM.

HEY KID. LET ME SEE YOUR GLASSES.

MY LAST PAIR OF CONTACTS RIPPED.

CAN I HAVE--

SHOVE!

THESE ARE CLOSE ENOUGH. THANKS, SQUIRT.

WHY'D YOU LET HIM TAKE YOUR GLASSES?

HE JUST TOOK THEM.

YOU CAN'T JUST LET THEM DO STUFF LIKE THAT. YOU CAN'T JUST BE A WIMP, PRABIR!

I'LL-- I'LL JUST ASK FOR THEM BACK. POLITELY.

WHERE YOU GOING? GUYS!

I GOT THEM FROM THAT INDIAN KID. HOW DO I LOOK?

YOU LOOK LIKE... LIKE A TOOL. HEH.

OH IS THAT RIGHT?

EXCUSE ME SIR, I KIND OF NEED THOSE.

PRABIR, YOU CAN'T JUST ASK. HE'S NOT GOING TO DO IT IF YOU JUST ASK.

I TOLD YOU I'D GIVE THEM BACK.

NO YOU DIDN'T. YOU JUST TOOK THEM.

HE NEEDS THEM! GIVE THEM BACK!

I'M GOING TO STOMP YOUR FACE INTO THE FLOOR, YOU LITTLE PUNK.

YOU HAVE NO IDEA WHAT I'M CAPABLE OF.

HEY!

WHAT'S GOING ON?

NONE OF US WANT ANY TROUBLE. WHY ARE YOU TRYING TO START SOME?

I MEAN COME ON DUDE, DON'T BE A TURD.

FINALLY.

JUST LET HIM BORROW YOUR GLASSES.

WAIT-- WHAT?

DO IT!

WHAT'S GOING ON?

SORRY BILL, THE KIDS WERE GETTING A LITTLE BIG FOR THEIR BRITCHES. I THINK I GOT IT UNDER CONTROL.

THAT'S NOT COOL, TRAVIS!

COME ON. GET UP, PRABIR.

SOMEBODY HIT THE JACKPOT TODAY!

YOU'RE WALKING TALL, STEVE. TALLER, AT LEAST. FOUND YOURSELF A FIREARM, I SEE.

CHECK THIS! 30.06, HIGH POWERED BIG GAME RIFLE. IT SHOOTS ARMOR PIERCING, TRACER ROUNDS. IT'S AGAINST THE GENEVA CONVENTION TO SHOOT A HUMAN BEING WITH THIS GUN.

YOU KNOW WHAT THIS MEANS, STEVE?

WHAT DOES THIS MEAN, BILL?

YOU DON'T NEED THAT TASER ANYMORE, DO YOU?

HAND IT OVER TO OUR NEW FRIEND.

OH MAN, THIS IS AWESOME.

THE THING WITH THIS GUN, YOU HAVE TO BE A TOTAL CRACK SHOT LIKE ME TO--

STEVE, QUIET FOR A MOMENT. THIS IS IMPORTANT.

YOU GOTTA LEARN HOW TO USE IT, TRAVIS. NOTHING WORSE THAN SOME IDIOT RUNNING AROUND WITH A WEAPON HE HAS NO CLUE HOW TO USE.

THE ONLY WAY TO RESPECT A WEAPON IS TO HAVE USED IT. ANYONE WANT TO VOLUNTEER?

ASSISTANT TRIBE LEADER, DID I SEE YOUR ARM GO UP?

WHAT? I DIDN'T--

HE HAS TO LEARN HOW TO USE IT.

CAN'T WE JUST TRACK DOWN A MUTANT OR LIKE A RABID SQUIRREL?

NAH KID, YOU GOTTA LEARN TO USE A TOOL RIGHT. AND THIS...

...IS AN IMPORTANT TOOL.

YOU JUST POINT AND SHOOT.

TRAVIS, WHAT ARE YOU DOING?

THIS IS WRONG.

IT'S ALL RIGHT. I'VE BEEN TASERED BEFORE.

I DON'T WANT--

COME ON, TRAVIS. YOU A BOY OR ARE YOU ONE OF US?

TRAVIS. TRAVIS, IT'S OKAY.

CRACK

ZZZT!

AAAAHHH!

I'M GOING TO KILL TRAVIS. I'M GOING TO--

DID YOU SEE HIM TWITCH?!

HE DID WHAT HE THOUGHT HE NEEDED TO. TRAVIS IS... TRAVIS.

WHY WOULD HE DO THAT?

YEAH, THAT FELT JUST LIKE I REMEMBERED IT FROM TRAINING. I DIDN'T PEE MYSELF, DID I?

NOT THAT I CAN TELL.

ANYONE WANNA GO UP TO THE ROOF AND WATCH ME BLOW THE HEADS OFF SOME SICKOS?

ANYONE?

HERE'S THE THING! JUST CUZ I GOT THIS DOESN'T MEAN I'M BETTER THAN YOU. BILL AIN'T BETTER THAN ME! I KNOW IT!

STOMP

THUMP

CRACK

SKF

SPIT

TAK

CRASH! ZZZT!

WE NEED TO JUST WALK OUT.

WALK WHERE?

HOME! I HAVEN'T SEEN MY HOUSE, YET. MY FOLKS MIGHT BE BARRICADED IN.

LUCAS... THERE'S SOMETHING--

MY BROTHER--

WHO CARES ABOUT YOUR BROTHER?! HE'S A JERK! HE COST PRABIR HIS GLASSES! HE TASERED BUDDY! HE'S BEEN SITTING ON HIS BUTT THE WHOLE TIME.

HIS PLAN TO GET US OUT OF HERE WAS JUST LIES!

TINK

TINK
TINK
TINK
TINK
TINK
TINK

GUYS...

WE'RE SUPPOSED TO GO TO THE PARKING LOT NOW.

LET GO OF MY WRIST, BILL.

NO.

WHERE'S THAT FAT KID? HE WAS IN CHARGE OF THE GENERATOR.

I DON'T KNOW, BILL, BUT WE'RE LEAVING. YOU CAN'T KEEP US HERE.

PLEASE, DON'T LET BUDDY GET KILLED.

THERE HE IS. YOU--

BANG

IS THAT BILL? HE SHOT BILL...?

BRAH, WHAT DID YOU DO?

I'M RUNNING THIS FRANCHISE, NOW.

DON'T YOU EVEN *THINK* ABOUT GOING OUT THAT DOOR.

C'MON! MOVE IT, BRAVES!

BUDDY, YOU SHOULD DRIVE. THERE'S AN EXTRA PEDAL THERE THAT I HAVE NO IDEA WHAT IT DOES.

ON IT!

GET INSIDE! MUTANTS ARE COMING.

I HOPE SO.

SONGS OF THE JUNIOR BRAVES

by Mr. Benedict Smedberg, Esq.
Founder, Junior Braves
Known to American Indians as "Loyal Oak"

CALL AND RESPONSE SONGS

"Call and Response" songs are a form of interaction between the speaker and the listener, in which every utterance of the speaker elicits an audible response (often in the form of an echo) from the listener. In native cultures throughout the world, call-and-response songs are a revered and important form of group participation.

"THE BRAVE AND HIS BOW"

He sat on a hillside and strung his bow,
    He strung his bow.
He sat on a hillside and strung his bow.
    He strung his bow.

He heard her cry from the river below.
    River below.
He heard her cry from the river below.
    River below

(All together)
He got up and he went down.
    He got up and he went down.
Down in the river she thought she'd drown
    Down in the river she thought she'd drown

The Brave grabbed an arrow and a length of rope.
    A length of rope.
The Brave grabbed an arrow and a length of rope.
    A length of rope.

The girl in the river, he was her only hope.
    Her only hope.
The girl in the river, he was her only hope.
    Her only hope

(All together)
He loosed the arrow and away it flew.
    He loosed the arrow and away it flew.
Stuck in a tree, his aim was true.
    Stuck in a tree, his aim was true.

She grabbed the rope as she floated by.
    She floated by.
She grabbed the rope as she floated by.
    She floated by.

She'd love that Brave 'til the day she die.
    The day she die.
She'd love that Brave 'til the day she die.
    The day she die.

———

A wise Chief once told his people, *"The act of singing is a delight to nature, and good to preserve the health of a Brave. It strengthens all parts of the chest, and opens the pipes."*

The Junior Braves should use the songs in this section on any occasion that they wish to express joy and togetherness. On the darkest day, a song can lift the spirit higher than the wings of an eagle.

✕

"THERE WAS A BEAR"

The other day.
    The other day.
I met a bear.
    I met a bear.

Out in the woods.
    Out in the woods.
A-way out there.
    A-way out there.

(All together)
The other day I met a bear
Out in the woods a-way out there.

He said to me
    He said to me
Why don't you run?
    Why don't you run?
I see you ain't
    I see you ain't
Got any gun
    Got any gun.
And so I ran
    And so I ran
Away from there
    Away from there
But right behind
    But right behind
Me was that bear
    Was that bear

Ahead of me
    Ahead of me
I saw a tree
    I saw a tree
A great big tree
    A great big tree
Oh glory be
    Oh glory be

The nearest branch
    The nearest branch
Was 10 feet up
    Was 10 feet up
I'd have to jump
    I'd have to jump
And trust my luck
    And trust my luck

(All together)
The nearest branch was 10 feet up
I'd have to jump and trust my luck

And so I jumped
    And so I jumped
Into the air
    Into the air
But I missed that branch
    I missed that branch
Away up there
    Away up there
Now don't you fret
    Now don't you fret
Now don't you frown
Now don't you frown

Cause I caught that branch
    I caught that branch
On the way back down
    On the way back down
That's all there is
    All there is
There ain't no more
    Ain't no more

Unless I meet
    Unless I meet
That bear once more
    That bear once more

—

CHAPTER FIVE...

I AM AWESOME!

WHAT? MY PLAN WORKED! WE'VE GOT WHEELS AND GAS AND THERE'S NOTHING BETWEEN US AND FINDING OUR PARENTS.

WAS BEING AN ARROGANT JERK PART OF YOUR PLAN? TASERING BUDDY? HOW ABOUT PRABIR AND TAKING AWAY HIS GLASSES?

YEAH, IT WAS ACTUALLY. WELL, KINDA. AND PRABIR--

I'M SORRY. I NEEDED TO GET THEM TO TRUST ME.

HOW DID YOU GET THEM BACK?

I CONVINCED RANDY IT WAS THE RIGHT THING TO DO.

CHANCES ARE THIS PLACE WAS RAIDED BY EVERYONE HEADED WEST. I'M SURE THEY TOOK EVERYTHING.

THERE'S PROBABLY SOME FOOD IN THE BACK, RIGHT?

ULP.

BLOOOORSH!!

MARVIN, WHY DID YOU DO THAT?

IT SAID 'TRY ME!'

LET'S GET BACK TO THE-- UH-OH.

SPECIAL DELIVERY, MR. MCFEELY.

CLICK

ARGH!

SHUFFLE SHUFFLE

I JUST STABBED SOMEONE!

GAH!

I'VE NEVER STABBED ANYONE BEFORE.

IT WAS A ZOMBIE, NOT A PERSON.

I THINK THEY LEFT.

THE SHOTGUN WAS EMPTY! BILL RAN THAT PLACE WITH AN EMPTY GUN!

AN EMPTY GUN!

WHOA.

THAT'S A BIG ONE.

LUCAS KILLED IT!

I HAD TO!

SMACH

POP SSSSHHH!

KA-CHUNK

THERE GOES THE VAN.

THEY WRECKED THE VAN? WHY?

WHAT DO YOU MEAN, WHY?

THEY'RE NOT SMART, ARE THEY? THEY SHOULD STILL BE COMING AFTER US, NOT OUR CAR.

THEY'RE MONSTERS.

THEY USED TO BE PEOPLE, THOUGH.

I FOLLOWED YOUR TRAIL MARKERS, OF COURSE.

THOUGH I DID LOSE YOU TWO DAYS AGO.

WE DIDN'T LEAVE TRAIL MARKERS.

WELL, I DREW ONE ON THE SIDE OF THE VAN ON THE FIRST NIGHT. THEN I LEFT A ROCK MARKER ON THE PORCH AND A SIGN ON THE DOOR AT OUR HOUSE AND THEN ANOTHER AT THE FIRE STATION AND THEN ONE WITH ROCKS AT THE SCHOOL, BUT THEN WE GOT SIDE-TRACKED.

WE WERE SUPPOSED TO START GOING WEST, REMEMBER?

GOOD THINKING, DORKUS.

BUT-- BUT--

DO YOU KNOW WHAT HAPPENED?

I--I DON'T KNOW WHAT HAPPENED TO THE TOWN.

I JUST DON'T KNOW.

PADRE... WHERE'S DYLAN?

...

GUYS, GO TAKE A LOOK AT THE VAN AND SEE WHAT SUPPLIES WE HAVE LEFT.

BUDDY, YOU KEPT THEM ALIVE. YOU DID GOOD, REAL GOOD.

THOSE BOYS KEPT THEMSELVES ALIVE. I HOPE TO GOD THERE'S SOMETHING FOR THEM WHEREVER WE END UP.

I... NEVER LOST A KID BEFORE. I DON'T EVEN KNOW WHAT I'D SAY TO THE BOY'S MOTHER AND FATHER.

WHAT HAPPENED TO YOU? Y'KNOW, SINCE THE CHURCH?

CHASED SOME OF THEM THAT I THOUGHT HAD DYLAN. THEY DIDN'T. IT WAS LIKE HE VANISHED... BEEN ON YOUR TRAIL UNTIL I LOST IT. THEN I SEARCHED EVERYONE'S HOUSES.

AH-HA, I KNEW I SMELLED IT.

IT'S GOING TO BE ABOUT THE SMALL THINGS FROM NOW ON.

RON, DID YOU SEE LUCAS' HOUSE?

...YOU DON'T SAY A DAMN WORD. NOT ONE.

HOLD STILL.

IT STINGS. AM I THE ONLY ONE BLEEDING?

MARVIN, DON'T CRY. THIS IS GOING TO HURT, BUT JUST FOR LIKE A MINUTE... OR TWO. MAYBE THREE.

IT HURTS NOW!

IT'S GOING TO HURT, OKAY?

TRAVIS! OWWWWW!

I DIDN'T EVEN WANT TO FIGHT THEM ANY MORE.

AMIR, DON'T SAY THAT. YOU'RE THE BEST! YOU'RE TOUGH! TO THE EIGHTH POWER TOUGH! NOW, KNOCK IT OFF!

LOOK ALIVE, 65! AS I SEE IT, WE CAN HEAD BACK TOWARD TOWN AND SEE IF WE CAN FIND ANOTHER VEHICLE.

PADRE, WE DON'T WANT TO GO BACK.

WITH EVERYTHING THAT CAN HAPPEN BACK THERE, I THINK WE SHOULD MOVE FORWARD. STAY AWAY FROM THE INTERSTATE AND TAKE THE OLD HIGHWAY. MAYBE FIND A VEHICLE ALONG THE WAY.

IT'S ABOUT 90 MILES TO SEATTLE. THAT'S WHERE WE THINK EVERYONE WAS EVACUATED TO.

HIKE ALL THE WAY TO SEATTLE? THAT'S MIGHTY BRAVE OF YOU.

DAY 11.

THE JUNIOR WILL

ZACH LEHNER graduated from the Savannah College of Art and Design in 2008 with a B.A. in Sequential Art and again with a Masters in 2010. This is his first graphic novel. He lives in northern Chicago, where he reads a lot of books. You can see more of his work at zlehner.com and on Twitter at @zlehner.

Zach would like to thank his family for their patience and support. Thanks also to Patty Reese, who always said this would happen, and asked to be mentioned when it did.

———

GREGORY K. SMITH grew up in a culturally diverse working class household. He was smitten with books at an early age when his assistant librarian mother brought him to work during summer breaks. Later, his father got him into Boy Scouts, where he achieved Eagle Scout Rank.

At some point, a good teacher or two told Greg he should write. So he took more classes and he wrote. He wrote a lot. He met Mike in one of those classes. They wrote more together. They found a cool dude named Zach and he drew the things. Now, the three

MICHAEL TANNER was born in Great Falls, Montana—a thriving metropolis that is actually smaller than the neighborhood of Los Angeles that he currently resides in. He has a BA in Theater and Television Production from the Evergreen State College, which is also where he met Greg Smith.

Michael developed a love for comics at a very early age and credits the medium with expanding his vocabulary and imagination. His first published comic work was in the Oni Press anthology *Jam! Tales from the World of Roller Derby.* He feels incredibly lucky to have been given the opportunity to work in a field that he loves.

He would like to dedicate this book to his parents who have always encouraged his endeavors, no matter how strange.

Follow Mike [and his LA Derby Dolls roller derby Enforcer alter ego] @mikeisernie, and check out his reviews of Los Angeles' best, worst, and weirdest diners at: *dinerwood.blogspot.com.*

—

of them make cool stuff with the AWESOME people at Oni Press!

Greg and his wife Anne live in the Pacific Northwest. They have two dogs and one cat. When not trying to turn their house into either "Pee-wee's Playhouse," "Double Dare Challenge," or "Mini Museum," they can be found at toy shows, comic shops, and thrift stores wherever they travel.

Follow Greg and his life adventures on Twitter and Instagram at @ThatAmazingTwit, or Tumblr at thatamazingtwit.tumblr.com

—

FOLLOW BOTH MIKE & GREG ON TWITTER @2AMAZINGWRITERS

MORE BOOKS FROM ONI PRESS

**SCOTT PILGRIM, VOL. 1:
PRECIOUS LITTLE LIFE**
By Bryan Lee O'Malley
192 pages, Hardcover, Color
ISBN 978-1-62010-000-4

METEOR MEN
By Jeff Parker and Sandy Jarrell
136 pages, Softcover, Color
ISBN 978-1-62010-151-3

**COSTUME QUEST: INVASION
OF THE CANDY SNATCHERS**
By Zac Gorman
56 pages, Hardcover, Color
ISBN 978-1-62010-190-2

**BAD MACHINERY, VOL. 1: THE CASE
OF THE TEAM SPIRIT**
By John Allison
136 pages, Softcover, Color
ISBN 978-1-62010-084-4

BLACK METAL: OMN1BVS
By Rick Spears and Chuck BB
472 pages, Softcover, B&W
ISBN 978-1-62010-143-8

ORPHAN BLADE
By M. Nicholas Almand
and Jake Myler
192 pages, Softcover, Color
ISBN 978-1-62010-120-9

PRESS
www.onipress.com

For more information on these and other fine Oni Press comic books and graphic novels visit www.onipress.com.
To find a comic specialty store in your area visit www.comicshops.us.